KLONDIKE GOLD

by Alice Provensen

Simon & Schuster Books for Young Readers
New York   London   Toronto   Sydney

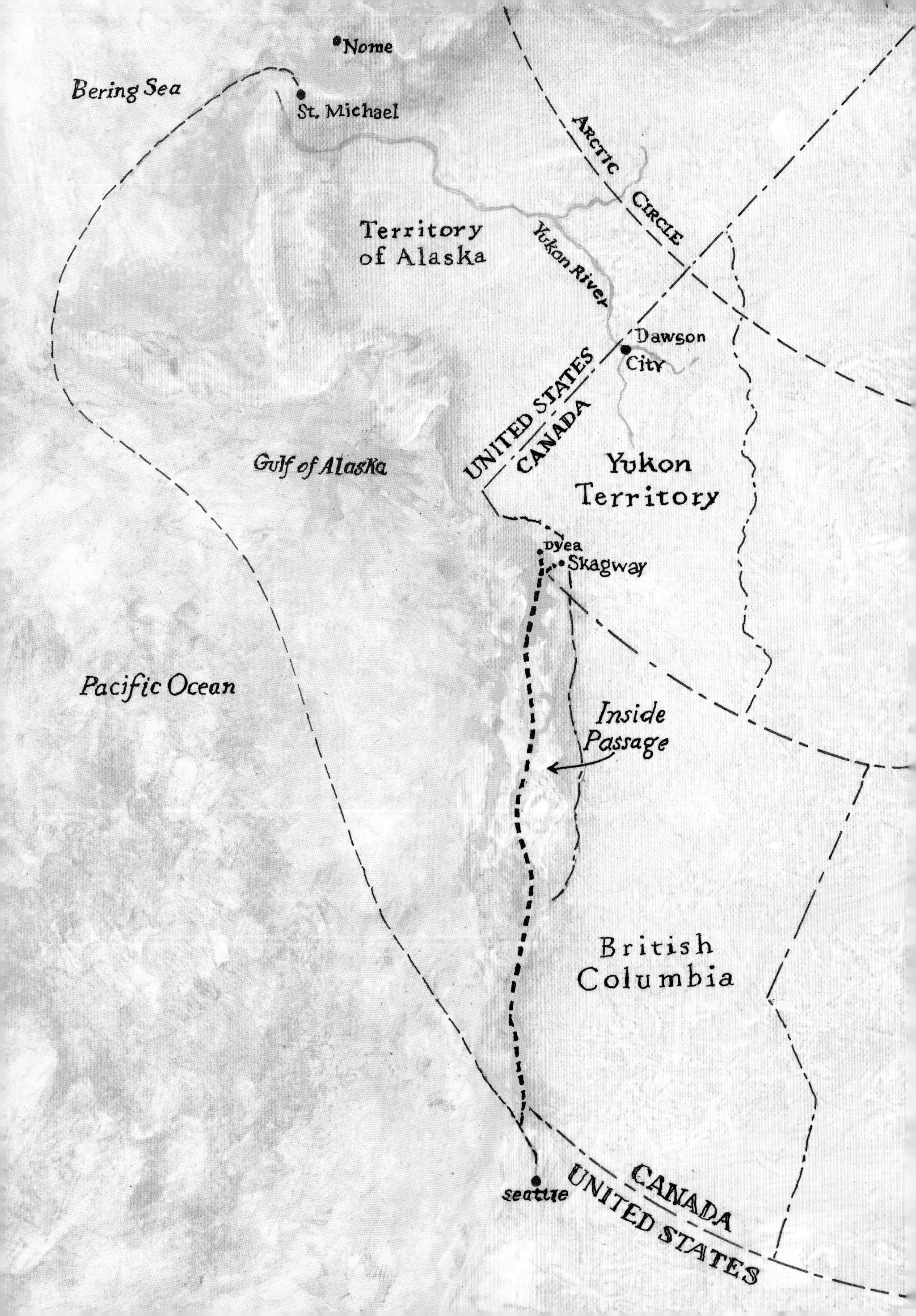

Bering Sea

Nome

St. Michael

Territory
of Alaska

Arctic Circle

Yukon River

Gulf of Alaska

UNITED STATES

CANADA

Dawson
City

Yukon
Territory

Dyea
Skagway

Inside
Passage

Pacific Ocean

British
Columbia

CANADA

Seattle

UNITED STATES

Introduction

More than a hundred years ago, a handful of eternally optimistic miners set off to prospect the Canadian Northwest Territories and our recently purchased wilderness, Alaska. They left the last decade of the nineteenth century, the so-called Gay Nineties, behind them. These were desperate years for most Americans. A great depression had settled over the country. Times were hard and jobs were scarce, if they existed at all. Mortgages were foreclosed, leaving families homeless and even starving. Just when all hope for the future seemed to be at an end, two ships from Alaska arrived on the West Coast.

The first one landed in San Francisco. A rusty old steamer, *Excelsior,* unloaded a score of ragged prospectors and a thousand pounds of gold. Two days later a much larger and even shabbier old ship, the *Portland,* docked in Seattle and unloaded two *tons* of gold. Her passengers, equally shabby, although some were waving top hats, assured the crowds already collecting on the dock that there was plenty more gold where that came from: the banks of the Klondike River (a tributary of the Yukon River). The news of the gold strike spread like wildfire.

Here was excitement! Here the thrilling promises of the get-rich-quick American myth: the royal flush, the winning lottery ticket, the unexpected inheritance. Here the sunken treasure ship, the winning horse, the pot at the end of the rainbow . . . GOLD! "Yukon Fever" infected people from all over the world. Of the tens of thousands of Americans who said they were going one hundred thousand actually left their homes and traveled to the gold fields. Among them was a young man named Bill Howell.

Bill had been raised on a sheep farm in southern Vermont, but he hated farming and he thought sheep were dumb. In despair, Bill was sent to school in Boston to learn a trade. Trades didn't interest Bill. Instead he let his mind wander in the streams and fields of literature, journals of travel and adventure. Finally he took a dull job in a dry-goods store to support himself. When Bill heard of all that gold, no one was surprised when he wandered away to find it.

This is his story.

On a gray, dismal day in spring, I had nearly fallen asleep in the shop where I worked. There hadn't been a customer all day and I had begun to think there never would be one. I felt fretful and ill-humored, as well as hopelessly bored, when suddenly the door flew open and startled me out of my doldrums. My friend Joe blew in on a tidal wave of energy and a blizzard of newspapers. He started shouting about the Klondike River, wherever that was, and a gold strike, and he was going, and would I go with him. I sure would! Anything but stay here.

Together we pored over the newspapers and the maps of the region. Joe was a few years older than I, and had been out West before, working in mines in California and Colorado. He returned to Boston without a lot of money but with a wealth of experience. He had lists of what we would need, he knew how to cook out-of-doors, and he knew how to keep warm. . . . Here was a dream come true! Without a backward glance we pooled what savings we had, bought two tickets to Chicago, and from there worked or bummed our way west on the freight trains bound for Seattle.

Joe and I were surprised to find Seattle was already swarming with recent arrivals: with farmers and businessmen, with poor people who wanted to be rich and rich people who wanted to be richer, and women and immigrants and natives of every race and color, adventurers all, lured by the glittering promises of gold. Hard times were over for the shopkeepers, the shipping companies, the hotels and boardinghouses, and the dance halls of Seattle. We rented a room in a boardinghouse and set about buying supplies for our trip north.

RECOMMENDED "OUTFIT" FOR A GOLD SEEKER · FOOD, TOOLS, AND CLOTHING

Flour 800 lbs	Evaporated Potatoes 50 lbs	30 Pounds of Nails	Baking Powder 20 lbs	Evaporated Peaches 50 lbs	Rice 100 lbs	Matches 25 lbs	Jamaica Ginger 3 lbs	2 Pocket Knives
Bacon 300 lbs		Pilot Bread 50 lbs	Tea 25 lbs	2 Draw Knives	Ground Pepper 3 lbs	3 Chisels, assorted	2 Hunting Knives	1 Whipsaw
Butter, hermetically sealed 40 lbs	2 Shovels	Roast Coffee 50 lbs	Evaporated Apples 50 lbs	Baking Soda 6 lbs	Evaporated Vinegar 12 lbs	Split Peas 50 lbs	2 Hatchets	1 Caulking Iron
1 Handsaw	Rolled Oats 80 lbs	Beef Extract 3 lbs	2 Handled Axes	Salt 40 lbs	1 Brace and 4 Bits	Ginger 2 lbs	6 Towels	2 Heavy Flannel Overshirts
Cornmeal 50 lbs	Dry Salt Pork 50 lbs	1/2 Dozen assorted Files	Yeast Cakes 6 lbs	Evaporated Apricots 50 lbs	Beans 200 lbs	Candles, 2 boxes 80 lbs	3 Heavy Suits Underwear	2 Pairs Blankets
Dried Beef 60 lbs	Evaporated Onions 20 lbs		Condensed Milk 50 lbs	1 Jack Plane	Ground Mustard 2 lbs	2 Butcher Knives	2 Pairs Overalls	2 Compasses

I don't think I had really realized until then that the Klondike River was in Canada, or that anyone crossing into the Canadian Northwest Territories was required to bring a year's supply of food, medicine, clothing, and tools. Joe, having read up on these matters, made most of the decisions as to what would be needed. My enthusiasm rose as we outfitted ourselves and fell when I thought of how much it must all weigh. But we were strong and young and felt prepared to challenge the elements and embrace the hardships and weight of the future.

2 Scissors Knives and Forks	Fish Lines and Hooks	2 Bread Pans	1 Pair Mackinaw Pants	4 Pairs All-Wool Mittens	6 Pairs Long Knit Socks	2 Pair Stockings, leather heels	1 Pair Hip Boots	2 Pairs Rubber Shoes
1 Heavy Mackinaw Over-Coat	2 Large Spoons	1 Mackinaw Coat, extra heavy	1 Extra Heavy Packing Bag	1 Suit Oil Clothing and Hat	1 Doz. Bandanna Kerchiefs	1 Canvas Sleeping Bag	2 Prospector's Picks	2 Grub Bags
1 Fur Cap	1 All-Wool Sweater	1 Pair Leather Suspenders	15 Pounds of Pitch	20 Pounds of Oakum	2 Gold Pans	4 Galvanized Pails	1 Whetstone	2 Picks and Handles
1 Set Awls and Tools	1 Wool Scarf	1 Medicine Case	1 Measuring Tape	2 Money Belts	2 Cartridge Belts	2 Gold-dust Bags	2 Pairs Snow Glasses	1 Camp Kettle
	150 Feet of Rope	1 Chalk Line	Granite Plates	2 Coffee Pots	2 Frying Pans	1 Stove (Yukon)	4 Granite Buckets	
	1 Gold Scale	Granite Cups						

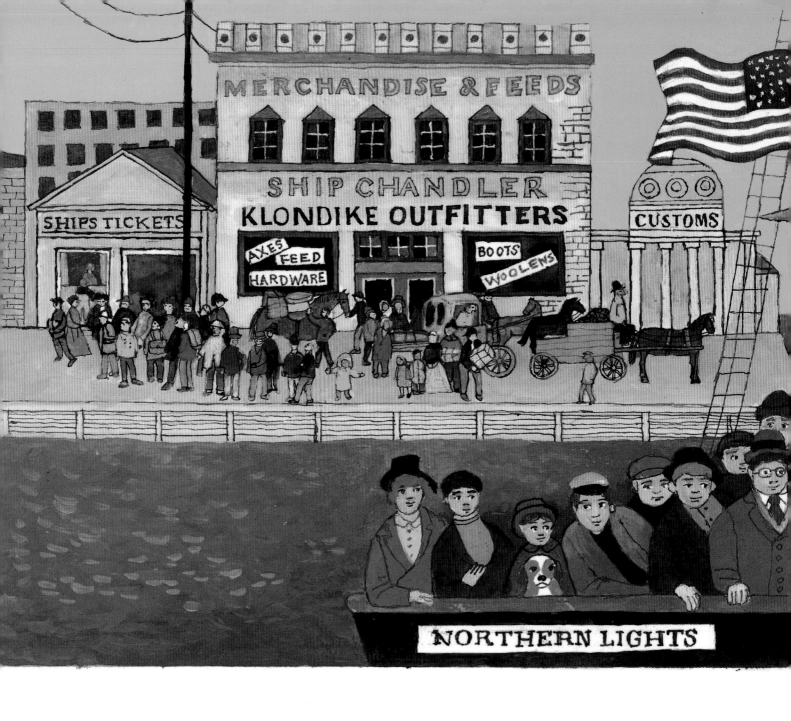

There were three ways to get where we wanted to go. The most comfortable way was to sail around the Alaskan Peninsula to Saint Michael, then up the Yukon to Dawson. We decided it was too far (4,200 miles), and too time-consuming (forty days) and far too expensive for our budget. Alternatively we could sail north from Seattle to Juneau, then through the Inside Passage to either Dyea and the Chilkoot Trail, or Skagway and the White Pass into Canada. Joe and I decided to disembark at Dyea. The trail was six hundred feet higher, but the trek to the border was ten miles shorter.

We bought the last two tickets on the steamer *Northern Lights* bound for Alaska. How happy I was on the day we sailed! Once underway a strange moody silence fell over all the ship's passengers. We looked at each other with the realization that we were going to a place cut off from the rest of the world for most of the year; not knowing how long we would be gone, on a project with no guarantee of success, or promise of a safe return. As we sailed between the islands of the Inside Passage and up the Lynn Canal, the most beautiful coastline I had ever seen, my mood lightened.

It was when we reached Dyea that our difficulties began. There were no docks or piers. We anchored a mile from shore at low tide. We passengers and our luggage were loaded onto barges and ferried to shore. The horses and dogs were dumped overboard into the sea to fend for themselves. We all had to move off the beach before the tide came in. But many a man lost all his goods as well as his dreams when the tide went out and they were washed back out to sea. Joe and I could neither afford a wagon, nor did we have any dogs to take us to the base of the mountain.

Skagway had piers and wharves and supposedly an easy trail to the White Pass.

So we and most of the rest of the passengers carried our supplies on our backs, making several trips in the process. Faced with slime and shale and mushy snow, sliding and falling we stumbled up to the base of the trail. Exhausted, we built a fire of tree stumps, lined our tent with pine branches and, after a dinner of beans, lay down and slept like stones. Our first campsite in Alaska! The next day, in a heavy snow, we dragged our loaded sleds through the desolate Dyea valley. We constantly met men who were turning back, not willing to brave such hardships for all the gold in the Yukon Territory.

Every community at the base of the Klondike started as a tent town. Within two months they were thriving boomtowns.

Refreshed, we were up early and on our way. We would pack as much as we could carry on our sleds and backs, go as far as we could, rest a little while, then return for another load from our cache. Thus we hiked forty miles to get ten miles closer to our goal. Sheep Camp was the next to the last staging area on the way to the Canadian border and only four miles from it. It was hard to believe it had taken twenty-three days to lug two tons of supplies thirteen miles. We settled down for a hot meal and a good visit with our fellow travelers whom we had met before on the boat or in Seattle.

The miners had their own courts of law. A standard punishment for a thief who stole a bag of sugar was fifty lashes, meted out by the injured party.

We felt relaxed in spite of the bedlam that surrounded us, sweating men, howling dogs, and abandoned horses. It was here we first heard rumors of the disasters on the White Pass Trail and we felt smug about our decision to brave the Dyea Trail instead. We bought candy and nuts and firewood. The women sang songs around the campfire until bedtime, when we all crept into our sturdy tents and pulled our warm blankets over our heads. During the night the temperature dropped to eighteen degrees below zero, followed by a raging blizzard that blanketed us with freezing snow.

One night sixty men were killed in an avalanche. The survivors dug out their supplies and "dug in" their dead. The women cared for the wounded.

Horses could not scramble beyond Sheep Camp and were left behind. From there on it was backpacking all the way to the Chilkoot Pass. Joe and I made forty trips to get our outfit that far and the last seven hundred feet of the climb seemed to be almost straight up. Stairs had been cut in the iciest part, and an endless line of men were working their way to the top. If one of them got out of line to rest for a minute it was almost impossible for him to get back in. It was equally hard to get down those icy stairs. Luckily, there was a shortcut back to the bottom.

The White Horse Trail was narrow and steep—a nightmare. The fodder brought for the horses had been used and there was no place to graze. When the starving horses stumbled and fell, their owners abandoned them.

Two women had almost made it to the top when they slipped and fell. In less time than it takes to tell it, they slid all the way to the bottom on their backsides. They gathered some more baggage and got back in at the end of the line again. Soon all the men had sewn patches on their trousers and had slid down too. When we stopped at the border to catch our breath Joe slapped me on the back. "Well, we made it this far," he said, "Now we'll see what Canada has to offer!" *It couldn't get worse,* I thought sourly, but I soon cheered up. It was hard to remain grumpy when Joe was so enthusiastic.

Cluttered with cached goods, useless sleds, and hundreds of dead and dying animals and despairing men, the way became known as the Dead Horse Trail.

At the summit, while waiting to have our supplies checked and weighed again, I had a chance to look around. Everything was on such a huge scale. Cut off from the world this way I felt like a tiny atom among these mighty snow-capped mountains and vast somber skies. At the same time it was exhilarating to be able to see so far in every direction. I could easily see the first frozen lake on our way north and the roiling water of the streams flowing into it. Now loaded up again we let our sleds run ahead of us down the slope into the Canadian Northwest Territories.

In all, thirty thousand men, women, and children crossed over the Chilkoot Pass into Canada. From the time they crossed the border until they left the country they were under the sole jurisdiction and protection of the Canadian Northwest Mounted Police. On the shores of the nearby frozen lakes thousands of tents were raised. Needing wood for fires and planks for boat building, the stampeders quickly denuded the hills of trees. A few months later these great tent cities had vanished forever.

At the base of the slope we gathered our loose belongings. We cached what we couldn't carry to be picked up later. We rigged sails made of blankets, tarps, and petticoats on our sleds and sped off toward Lake Lindeman. With a load of twelve hundred pounds we covered the ten miles in forty minutes! "This is more like it!" I hollered happily. Some men, too tired after their arduous tramp over the pass to go farther, decided to camp here. Others went on to Lake Bennett. Joe and I decided to go as far as Lake Tagish. The trail was not too difficult as trails go, and we would be nearly seventy miles closer to the Yukon River.

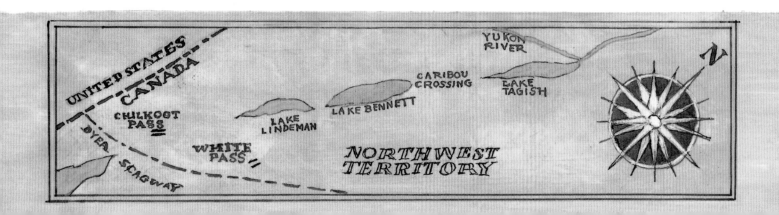

We had traveled only sixty miles from Dyea when we decided to stop to build our boat at Lake Tagish. Even though we were still more than five hundred miles from Dawson and the Klondike, it was a good decision. The location was fine for camping purposes. Other gold seekers were building boats there too, so we did not lack for company and advice, and most important, there still were plenty of trees for firewood and lumber. The worst seemed to be over for a time, I thought, as we sat before our little stove eating flapjacks as fast as we could cook them.

Working alongside of the men, the women seemed glad to be free of polite society's

Not that we did a lot of cooking. The whole Yukon must have smelled of bacon and beans (our everyday diet). But once in a while a woman would share a piece of cake with us. One of every ten stampeders was a woman; either the wife of a miner or women who had banded together to look for gold, employment and/or a husband. In general I didn't find them very attractive, but I have to say they were gallant. They hauled their own packs up the treacherous trail, they fetched water, built fires, baked bread, and tended the sick.

restraints and soon were to trade their impractical skirts for bloomers or men's trousers.

The source of the Yukon was still so far away I was happy to stop for a while to collect my wits. Looking back I realized we hadn't done so badly. We had had no major disasters. We hadn't been ill. We hadn't been injured. Our main occupation during the winter would simply be sawing wood into boards and building boards into boats. Joe, with his cheerful disposition and endless enthusiasm for new projects, hurled himself into his boat-building mode. In the morning we were introduced to our first bit of carpentry. Talk about "worst comes to first!"

The boats were ready before the river was.

There was never a more devilish device than a whipsaw. A whipsaw is used by two men on a platform strong enough to support a log, and as many feet long as can be managed. One man on top of the platform and the other underneath saw the log vertically up and down, and up and down, again and again, until the log has been cut through lengthwise. Joe and I almost ended our friendship making boards. With sawdust in our eyes, and our throats sore from shouting at each other, we quit work for a while to nurse our blistered hands and perhaps to sulk a little before shaking hands again.

They looked surprisingly seaworthy, all things considered, but they weren't ice boats. To stand around waiting for the river ice to break was maddening for the eager stampeders.

On May 29 we were startled awake by a powerful rumble and then a roar! The river ice had broken. Forgotten were the long cold nights, the below-zero weather, and the grim climb over the Chilkoot Pass. It was SPRING! We began to sing as we readied our boats for the long trip down the Yukon. That day eight hundred boats were launched. Within forty-eight hours 7,124 boats followed. Skiffs and scows, canoes and kayaks, boats of canvas and boats of balsa—boats screwed together and boats glued together, boats that looked like boxes and boats that looked like coffins, all hoisted sails, all with one destination, Dawson and the gold fields!

Many boats foundered or broke up in the rapids. Many men drowned.

The Yukon proved at once that it was a mighty river. It had high, narrow canyons enclosing it, unstable embankments falling into it, and giant boulders cluttering its icy cold water. A constant high wind whistled above it. At one point Joe and I landed onshore to debate the best way of crossing the upcoming rapids. Some men portaged their boats and goods; some men emptied their boats and ran the rapids empty. Naturally, Joe was for a head-on attack. True to form, I shrieked when I saw the first tumultuous current. It turned us backward and downward in a horrifying way, but somehow we landed right side up and going downstream in the right direction.

Then thanks to the river gods, it was clear sailing all the rest of the way.

Autumn found Joe and me among the first of that crazy flotilla to tie up at Dawson Docks. You can't imagine the elation we had felt as we rounded a bend in the river and got our first glimpse of Dawson City. We hugged each other and jumped up and down almost capsizing our boat. After us, boats arrived day and night without letup for more than a month. Each passenger landed excited and proud; excited to be alive and proud of having been able to get here. And here they were! Dawson! Front Street was a row of unfinished buildings, logs, and sawn lumber and ultimately thirty million tons of food in transit.

In 1896 Dawson was a moose meadow with a town of twenty-nine people: twenty-seven men and two women. Two years later it was the second largest city in Canada with a fluctuating population of thirty to fifty thousand.

Oddly enough, the atmosphere became that of an aimless crowd without energy. Where was the gold? It certainly wasn't rolling around on the ground. It was as if having reached Dawson their mission had been accomplished. But what was there to celebrate? After the difficult and dangerous time getting here, the idea of gold lying in thirty feet of muck on some unknown riverbed was quite unacceptable. But not to Joe. He wasn't going to walk despondently up and down Front Street. We packed up our food and belongings and joined the *real* fortune hunters. Off to the Klondike!

The Royal Canadian Mounted Police administered Dawson. No handguns were allowed, no obscenity, no cheating, no risqué or seditious performances, no work on Sundays. The punishment: hard labor on the police woodpile or banishment from the region.

SUPT. SAM STEELE

Joe and I left Dawson early without anyone paying particular attention to our departure and we got as far as the junction of Bonanza and Eldorado Creeks before nightfall. We made camp where miners were already working on their claims or looking for likely ones. Every few days prospectors would return, skidding and sliding and shouting joyously to announce a lucky find close to a discovery claim. They were all friendly and suggested where we might do the same. They seemed to think if there was any gold to be found, there would be enough for everybody.

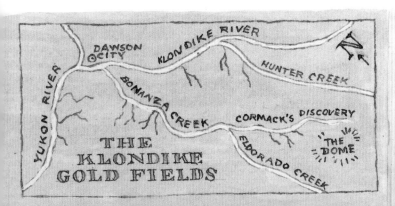

Prospectors had roamed over the Yukon Territory in search of gold for many years before George Cormack's Klondike discovery in 1896. His was the richest gold strike ever made. True to the "miners' code" he told others of his discovery. Within two weeks the entire length of the Bonanza Creek was claimed and prospectors began to seek out other sources. On nearby Eldorado Creek five men panned out more than a million dollars each from their five claims.

The Dominion Surveyors had limited the size of the claims to ten feet on either side of where the gold had been discovered and were numbered consecutively, number one up and number one down. All the claims had been spoken for on Bonanza Creek within two weeks. We hurried on. We finally found an open claim on Eldorado Creek that Joe thought promising and I agreed, not knowing anything about what he saw in it. He had no explanation, he just felt good about it. We now had to register our frozen bit of earth with the claims office and pay a fee for one year's use of it.

This is what stampeding was about. The chances of finding an original strike and getting rich were far less than getting rich by staking a claim adjoining a proven one. Cormack started one hundred thousand Americans on the scramble for gold and changed the history of Alaska, Western Canada, and the Pacific Northwest.

We decided to register this claim rather than search further. In any case, no one could possibly estimate its value before it was worked. We returned to camp and like the others before us, flung ourselves down the mountain grasping at underbrush and sending stones echoing down the hills, faster and faster. The men going out to look for a claim for the first time yelled at us, "How was it?" They wanted to know.

"Great!" we answered. "Ten dollars to the pan right out of the sand of the creek, but you'd better hurry, the claims are filling up fast."

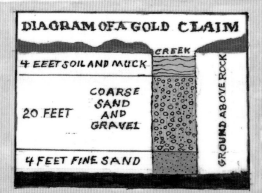

DIAGRAM OF A GOLD CLAIM

4 FEET SOIL AND MUCK

CREEK

COARSE SAND AND GRAVEL

20 FEET

GROUND ABOVE ROCK

4 FEET FINE SAND

The shining Eldorado—the richest creek in the Klondike watershed! Its gold was found in unexpected places. Even the most amateurish miner had as much a chance of striking it rich as the most experienced. Called placer mining, nuggets of gold were being taken from the rough surface of the shores of the creek and panned out of the sand on its edges, but this didn't mean there would be any at bedrock.

As it turned out, staking a claim was the easy part. Getting the gold out was the problem. Before we even knew if our claim was a good one or not, we spent a lot of money. So much for a rude hut (labor and wood), so much for timber for sluice boxes and keeping them set all summer, a waste ditch, and all those dozens of indispensable tools: wheelbarrows, shovels and a portable forge, axes, handsaws, a gold scale, and quicksilver to tell the temperature. After all, gold didn't grow on bushes. It had to be laboriously dug up, no easy task in the dead of winter when the temperature hovers between forty and fifty below.

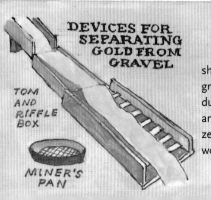

DEVICES FOR SEPARATING GOLD FROM GRAVEL

TOM AND RIFFLE BOX

MINER'S PAN

To find out what a claim was really worth, it was necessary to dig a shaft down to bedrock. Firewood had to be found for a fire to thaw the ground. Then a foot and a half of thawed muck, moss, and debris was dug up and piled to one side. This was repeated, thawing, shoveling, and hauling out the muck until the bedrock was reached. At fifty below zero the frozen piles could not be washed to separate the gold from the worthless earth until spring.

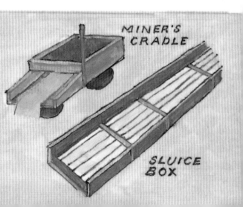

MINER'S CRADLE

SLUICE BOX

Now that we were all ready to start digging up gold we didn't loaf around the creeks congratulating ourselves. We headed back down the frozen Bonanza Creek to Dawson to register our claim and pay the fee for the use of our little piece of frozen land for one year. By this time Dawson was a full-blown city. It seemed very festive and we suddenly realized it was Christmas. Surprised, we awarded ourselves a small holiday. After attending to business, we picked up our newly washed and mended clothes, found a room for the night, then joined the crowd in the street. For Christmas we gave ourselves gifts of two trips to the bakery for freshly baked bread! A luxury.

We were also lucky enough to find a month-old newspaper. Now we could catch up on the news of the outside world. Everyone was celebrating something. The dance halls were crowded. The bars and the gambling houses were overflowing into the streets. The theaters gave ten performances that day. The music from the dance halls resounded in the streets. The women were as flirtatious as I was shy. Joe was not much for carousing either, so we fraternized with acquaintances made on the way here, and then went to bed. In the morning, refreshed in spirit, we started back up the slippery Bonanza to spend the New Year working on our own gold claim on Eldorado Creek.

We had already built a hut of green lumber but we found it was impossible to live in. The air became intolerable after we had filled the chinks to keep the cold out, so we sealed all the openings and used the hut for storage, then raised a big tent in front of it. The snow filled in all around it and protected us from the wind and we were comfortable. I, who had been apt to catch every cold that was going around Boston, didn't suffer even a sore throat all that long, dark winter when the temperature hovered in the minus sixties and the nights were twenty hours long.

The stars blazed overhead and the northern lights wobbled across the skies as we grubbed away underground hacking and hauling up tons of dirty gravel and dumping it on the ground. Or one of us was out searching for wood to keep our fires going. When we finally reached bedrock we drifted sideways. Here we met fellow prospectors who had done the same. We were not alone in wishing for an early spring when the creeks were running free and we could wash the winter's harvest of stones and earth, forcing it to yield up its treasure. It was only then that we would know whether or not we were rich or were even poorer than before.

We spent the spring and most of the summer washing the gold out of our piles of "pay dirt" and were gratified to see flakes and pebbles of pure gold captured in our sluice boxes, more than enough to fill the leather bags we had brought to carry it in. Joe estimated we would have fifty thousand dollars to divide between us, an amount that neither of us had ever seen or dreamed of. It made it hard to decide whether or not to spend another year in the Klondike working this claim, trying to find a better one, or to pack it in and go home. Most of the claims near us had already been abandoned or sold and the creeks had a desolate air about them.

The last passenger ship was dangerously overcrowded.

While we debated what to do we made a trip to Dawson to replenish our supplies only to find the city devastated. The stores were closed for lack of goods to sell. The lower Yukon was starting to freeze, so there would be no more supply ships to provide for the coming winter. The Canadian Mounties were predicting a famine and were offering the Americans enough provisions to get them out of the country if they could be persuaded to leave. We hated to sell our claim, but we got a decent price for it and decided to take the Mounties' offer while we could. We left for Eldorado to prepare for the trip home.

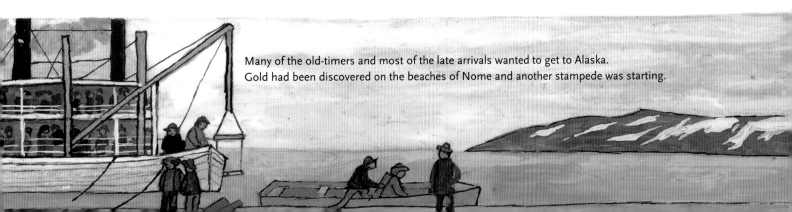

Many of the old-timers and most of the late arrivals wanted to get to Alaska.
Gold had been discovered on the beaches of Nome and another stampede was starting.

I thought we should go back the way we had come and for once Joe agreed with me. We knew the pitfalls of the trail back to Dyea and it couldn't be as hard to get back as it was to get here. I wanted to wait until the rivers were frozen and the trails were packed down, but Joe, as usual, was in a hurry. So we divided our gold evenly, split our possessions and loaded them on our sleds. I had my twenty-five thousand dollars, the food, the stove, two thin blankets, and some spare clothing. Joe packed the tents, the cooking utensils, our personal necessities, our sleeping bags, and his share of the gold, then started off hauling our overloaded sleds to Dyea.

Along the walls of the canyons was an uneven shelf of ice bordering the water. It was strong enough to hold us, but we came to a place where it slanted badly. To my horror I saw Joe slide off the embankment and into the stream. The sled sank instantly and Joe had to let it go lest he be pulled in after it. He was knee-deep in freezing water but somehow managed to scramble out, shivering with cold. I built a fire to dry him out and the minute he got warm he looked at me, burst into tears and cried like a baby. We had lost half our outfit and he all his money. I felt sorrier for him than I did for myself.

Joe was subdued after his scary experience. It was the first time I had ever seen him look helpless. I think everyone was changed by the Klondike. I know I was. I surprised myself when I offered half of my money to Joe.

The next day we took an inventory of the things we still had left. Happily, we had enough food to last us until we got to Dyea. We were grateful to the stampeders who were also leaving for the "outside," grateful for a little warmth at their campfires, and a night in a tent. The weather stayed fine as we trekked across the frozen lakes to the border at Chilkoot Pass. There a huge wind roused itself to remind us of what we were leaving behind. It blew us out of Canada, and dumped us into U.S. territory at the head of the Dyea Trail, now littered with broken sleds, horse skeletons, and adventurers' tombstones. The trip to Seattle was melancholy, but when I looked back at those somber shores and majestic mountains, I said, "We *could* come back next year."

Joe smiled.

For my daughter, Karen Mitchell

Author's Note

I am indebted to the authors of these three books for background and research on *Klondike Gold.*
Berton, Pierre. *The Klondike Quest: A Photographic Essay: 1897-1899,* Ontario: Boston Mills
Press, 1983.

Haskell, William B. (A Returned Gold Miner and Prospector), *Two Years in the Klondike and
Alaskan Gold-Fields, 1896–1898: A Thrilling Narrative of Life in the Gold Mines and Camps,*
vol. 5 of the University of Alaska Reprint Series, Fairbanks: University of Alaska Press, 1997.

Morgan, Murray. *One Man's Gold Rush: A Klondike Album,* photographs by E. A. Hegg,
Seattle: University of Washington Press, and Vancouver: Douglas & McIntyre, 1967.

I would like to thank my editor, David Gale; his assistant, Alexandra Cooper; and the book's
designer, Lucy Ruth Cummins, for their help and patience. I would also like to thank my friends
Linda Zuckerman, Maria Tucci, Nina Sommer, and Allelu Kurten for their encouragement.

SIMON & SCHUSTER BOOKS FOR YOUNG READERS · An imprint of Simon & Schuster Children's Publishing Division
1230 Avenue of the Americas, New York, New York 10020 · Copyright © 2005 by Alice Provensen
All rights reserved, including the right of reproduction in whole or in part in any form.
SIMON & SCHUSTER BOOKS FOR YOUNG READERS is a trademark of Simon & Schuster, Inc.
Book design by Lucy Ruth Cummins · The text for this book is set in Horley Old Style and Scala Sans.
The illustrations for this book are rendered in oils. · Manufactured in the United States of America
2 4 6 8 10 9 7 5 3 1
Library of Congress Cataloging-in-Publication Data · Provensen, Alice. · Klondike gold / Alice Provensen.— 1st ed. · p. cm.
Summary: A fictionalized account of William Howell, a young prospector who braved the arduous journey from Boston to the Yukon Territory
in search of gold in the Klondike River valley. · ISBN-13: 978-0-689-84885-8 · ISBN-10: 0-689-84885-4 (hardcover)
1. Howell, William, Prospector—Juvenile fiction. [1. Howell, William, Prospector—Fiction. 2. Gold mines and mining—Yukon Territory—
Fiction. 3. Yukon Territory—History—19th century—Fiction.] I. Title. · PZ7.P9457Kl 2005 · [Fic]—dc22   2004028405